Es un buen juego, querido dragón

It's a Good Game, Dear Dragon

por/by Margaret Hillert

ilustrado por/Illustrated by David Schimmell

NORWOOD HOUSE 🏠 PRESS

Queridos padres y maestros:

La serie para lectores principiantes es una colección de lecturas cuidadosamente escritas, muchas de las cuales ustedes recordarán de su propia infancia. Cada libro comprende palabras de uso frecuente en español e inglés y, a través de la repetición, le ofrece al niño la oportunidad de practicarlas. Los detalles adicionales de las ilustraciones refuerzan la historia y le brindan la oportunidad de ayudar a su niño a desarrollar el lenguaje oral y la comprensión.

Primero, léale el cuento al niño; después deje que él lea las palabras con las que está familiarizado y pronto, podrá leer solito todo el cuento. En cada paso, elogie el esfuerzo del niño para que se sienta más confiado como lector independiente. Hable sobre las ilustraciones y anime al niño a relacionar el cuento con su propia vida.

Sobre todo, la parte más importante de la experiencia de la lectura es ¡divertirse y disfrutarla!

Shannon Cannon

Shannon Cannon
Consultora de lectoescritura

Dear Caregiver,

The *Beginning-to-Read* series is a carefully written collection of readers, many of which you may remember from your own childhood. This book, *Dear Dragon's Day with Father*, was written over 30 years after the first *Dear Dragon* books were published. The *New Dear Dragon* series features the same elements of the earlier books, such as text comprised of common sight words. These sight words provide your child with ample practice reading the words that appear most frequently in written text. The many additional details in the pictures enhance the story and offer the opportunity for you to help your child expand oral language skills and develop comprehension.

Begin by reading the story to your child, followed by letting him or her read familiar words and soon your child will be able to read the story independently. At each step of the way, be sure to praise your reader's efforts to build his or her confidence as an independent reader. Discuss the pictures and encourage your child to make connections between the story and his or her own life.

Above all, the most important part of the reading experience is to have fun and enjoy it!

Shannon Cannon

Shannon Cannon,
Literacy Consultant

Norwood House Press • P.O. Box 316598 • Chicago, Illinois 60631
For more information about Norwood House Press please visit our website at *www.norwoodhousepress.com* or call 866-565-2900.
Text copyright ©2010 by Margaret Hillert. Illustrations and cover design copyright ©2010 by Norwood House Press, Inc. All rights reserved. No part of this book may be reproduced or utilized in any form or by any means without written permission from the publisher.
Designer: The Design Lab

LIBRARY OF CONGRESS CATALOGING-IN-PUBLICATION DATA

Hillert, Margaret.
   [It's a good game, dear dragon. Spanish & English]
   Es un buen juego, querido dragon = It's a good game, dear dragon / por Margaret Hillert ; ilustrado por David Schimmel ; traducido por Eida Del Risco.
      p. cm. -- (A beginning-to-read book)
   Summary: In this illustrated story told in both English and Spanish, a boy and his pet dragon play a game of soccer with friends and learn about sportsmanship.
   ISBN-13: 978-1-59953-362-9 (library edition : alk. paper)
   ISBN-10: 1-59953-362-6 (library edition : alk. paper)
   [1. Dragons--Fiction. 2. Soccer--Fiction. 3. Sportsmanship--Fiction. 4. Spanish language materials--Bilingual.] I. Schimmel, David, ill. II. Del Risco, Eida. III. Title. IV. Title: It's a good game, dear dragon. V. Title: It is a good game, dear dragon.
   PZ73.H557206 2010
   [E]--dc22
                                   2009041515

Manufactured in the United States of America in North Mankato, Minnesota. 161R-052010

Vamos. Vamos. Corre y toma la pelota.
Tenemos que ir al juego.

Come on. Come on. Run and get the ball.
We have to get to the game.

Sí, sí.
Aquí estoy.
Tengo la pelota.
Ahora nos podemos ir.

Yes, yes.
Here I am.
I have the ball.
We can go now.

Tú también vienes. Quiero que estés conmigo.
Puedes mirar lo que hago.
Juego con esta pelota. Es un buen juego.

You come, too. I want you with me.
You can see what I do.
I play with this ball. It is a good game.

Oh, mira.
Aquí está.
Este es el lugar
donde jugamos.

Oh, look here.
Here it is.
This is the spot where
we play the game.

Me gusta estar aquí. Qué gusto verte.
Nosotros somos los azules. Ustedes son los rojos.
Nos divertiremos.

It is good to be here. It is good to see you.
We are the blue ones. You are red.
We will have fun.

Tenemos que hacer esto
para poner la pelota en juego.

We have to do this
to put the ball in play.

Ahora, avanza, avanza, avanza.
Corre, corre, corre.

Now, go, go, go.
Run, run, run.

¡Y haz ESTO!

And do THIS!

Así. Así. Por aquí.
Queremos poner la pelota allá.

This way. This way. Down this way.
We want to get the ball down there.

Ahora mira esto.
La haré entrar.

Now see this.
I will make it go in.

Ay, no. No entró.

Oh, no. It did not go in.

¡Puedo hacer ESTO!

I can do THIS!

Oh, mira.
Tú también puedes hacerlo.
Eres un buen ayudante.

Oh, my.
You can do it, too.
You are a good help.

Allá vamos.
Corre, corre, corre.
Yo lo haré.

Here we go.
Run, run, run.
I will do it.

¡Cuidado!
¡Cuidado!

Look Out!
Look Out!

19

Ay, ay. Esto no está bien.
Pero vamos a levantarnos
y a jugar.

Oh, oh. This is not good.
But we will get up
and play.

Mira cómo avanzan.
Mira cómo avanzan.
Ay. Ay.

Look at them go.
Look at them go.
Oh, my. Oh, my.

Nosotros también avanzamos.
¡Corre, corre, CORRE-E-E-E!

Here we go, too.
Run, run, RUN-N-N!

¡Ay, no!
Ahora mira esto.
¿Ves esto?

Oh, no!
Now look at this.
Do you see this?

Ustedes son mejores que nosotros,
pero nosotros también somos buenos.
Fue un buen juego. Podemos ser amigos.
Podemos jugar y divertirnos.

You are too good for us,
but we are good, too.
It was a good game. We can be friends.
We can play and have fun.

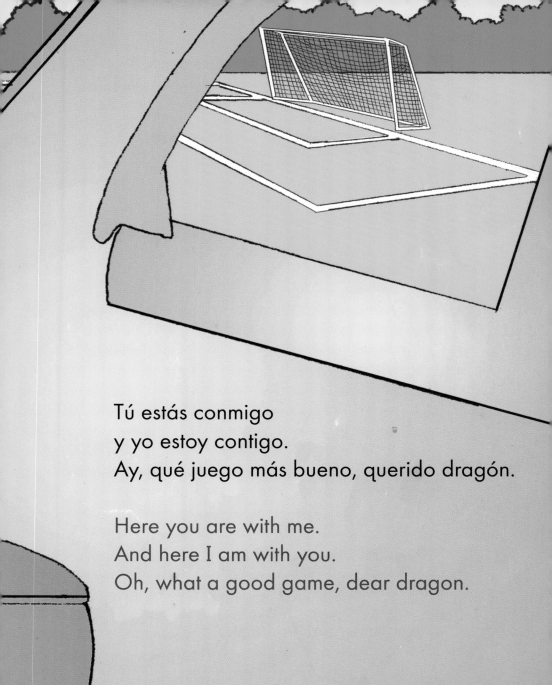

Tú estás conmigo
y yo estoy contigo.
Ay, qué juego más bueno, querido dragón.

Here you are with me.
And here I am with you.
Oh, what a good game, dear dragon.

READING REINFORCEMENT

The following activities support the findings of the National Reading Panel that determined the most effective components for reading instruction are: Phonemic Awareness, Phonics, Vocabulary, Fluency, and Text Comprehension.

Phonemic Awareness: Syllabication

Say the following words, clapping the syllables as you say them. Ask your child to tell you how many syllables are in each word:

play-1	ball-1	whistle-2	friend-1	soccer-2
happy-2	referee-3	winning-2	something-2	goalie-2
kick-1	breakfast-2	dragon-2	teammate-2	tipoff-2
children-2	trophy-2	mother-2		

Phonics: Syllabication

1. Write the following words on separate index cards:

soccer	little	running	jelly	supper
lesson	ladder	letter	silly	winning
happy	yellow	spotted	flipper	

2. Explain to your child that words that have two identical consonants in the middle are divided in between the two consonants.

3. Help your child cut each word in half between the double consonants.

Vocabulary: Movement Words

1. Write the following words on index cards and point to each card as you read the word to your child:

run	kick	pass	toss	scores	block

2. Rearrange the cards and say each word in random order and ask your child to point to the correct word as you say it.

3. Rearrange the cards again and ask your child to read as many as he or she can.

4. Say the following sentences aloud and ask your child to point to the word that is described:

- When the ball goes into the net the team _____ a point. (scores)

- Soccer players have to _____ fast to keep up. (run)

- At the beginning of the match, the referee will _____ a coin in the air to see who goes first. (toss)

- The goalie's job is to _____ the ball from getting into the net. (block)

- Sometimes players need to _____ the ball to other players to move the ball down the field. (pass)

- In soccer, the players _____ the ball to move it down the field because they cannot carry it. (kick)

Fluency: Choral Reading

1. Reread the story with your child at least two more times while your child tracks the print by running a finger under the words as they are read. Ask your child to read the words he or she knows with you.

2. Reread the story aloud together. Be careful to read at a rate that your child can keep up with.

3. Repeat choral reading and allow your child to be the lead reader and ask him or her to change from a whisper to a loud voice while you follow along and change your voice.

Text Comprehension: Discussion Time

1. Ask your child to retell the sequence of events in the story.

2. To check comprehension, ask your child the following questions:
    - Who is the adult wearing the whistle? What is his job?
    - What is happening on page 9? Why does this happen at the beginning of a soccer match? How does it make the game fair?
    - What is your favorite team sport to play or watch? Why?

Photograph by Glenna Washburn

ACERCA DE LA AUTORA

Margaret Hillert ha escrito más de 80 libros para niños que están aprendiendo a leer. Sus libros han sido traducidos a muchos idiomas y han sido leídos por más de un millón de niños de todo el mundo. De niña, Margaret empezó escribiendo poesía y más adelante siguió escribiendo para niños y adultos. Durante 34 años, fue maestra de primer grado. Ya se retiró, y ahora vive en Michigan donde le gusta escribir, dar paseos matinales y cuidar a sus tres gatos.

ABOUT THE AUTHOR

Margaret Hillert has written over 80 books for children who are just learning to read. Her books have been translated into many different languages and over a million children throughout the world have read her books. She first started writing poetry as a child and has continued to write for children and adults throughout her life. A first grade teacher for 34 years, Margaret is now retired from teaching and lives in Michigan where she likes to write, take walks in the morning, and care for her three cats.

ACERCA DEL ILUSTRADOR

David Schimmell fue bombero durante 23 años, al cabo de los cuales guardó las botas y el casco y se dedicó a trabajar como ilustrador. David ha creado las ilustraciones para la nueva serie de Querido dragón, así como para muchos otros libros. David nació y se crió en Evansville, Indiana, donde aún vive con su esposa, dos hijos, un nieto y dos nietas.

ABOUT THE ILLUSTRATOR

David Schimmell served as a professional firefighter for 23 years before hanging up his boots and helmet to devote himself to work as an illustrator. David has happily created the illustrations for the New Dear Dragon books as well as many other books throughout his career. Born and raised in Evansville, Indiana, he lives there today with his wife, two sons, a grandson and two granddaughters.